THE POWER OF THE JEDI....

No one remembers exactly who discovered the presence of the Force. According to one legend, Force sensitives from across the galaxy converged on the planet Tython where they became known as the Je'daii, a Dai Bendu term meaning "mystic center." At the beginning they were monks, thinkers, and scientists who started to study the mystical energy that they called the Force. In time they discovered that the Force offered almost infinite possibilities to those who learned to use it. Regarded as a source of both wisdom and power, the Force could be either a powerful tool or a dangerous weapon. In good times or in perilous times, the Force was always a great ally to those who guarded peace and justice in the galaxy—the righteous Jedi Knights.

THE FORCE SENSITIVES

The Force has always been in the universe. It binds the galaxy together, it surrounds and penetrates everything, and it's present in every living being. Those who can sense it quickly learn how to use it. Thanks to the Force they can be more agile, react quicker, move things without touching them, levitate, or even see the future. Some of the Force sensitives use their supernatural skills to do good, but some use them for evil purposes.

QUICK QUIZ

?! Q

The Force can be sensed by every living being in the galaxy. True or false?

MIDI-CHLORIANS

Midi-chlorians are intelligent, microscopic life-forms present in the cells of all living things. A being's potential in using the Force depended on a high midi-chlorian count in their blood. Anakin Skywalker had the highest known midi-chlorian count. With more than 20,000 midi-chlorians per cell, Anakin was attuned to the Force stronger than any Jedi.

LIGHT SIDE OF THE FORCE

Users of the Force choose to follow the light or the dark side of the Force. The light side is bound to life, harmony, peace, and knowledge. It requires patience, selflessness, and openness. The most dedicated followers of the light side of the Force were the members of the Jedi Order.

DARK SIDE OF THE FORCE

The dark side is more tempting for many users of the Force. It promises fast results in gaining powers beyond imagination. But the dark side feeds on anger, hatred, and selfishness. Its followers are obsessed with power and they always want more of it. The Sith were the most powerful dark siders.

THE JEDI ORDER

For thousands of years the Jedi were the guardians of peace in the galaxy. They solved conflicts using wisdom, logic, and tolerance. But when peaceful negotiations failed, the Jedi did not hesitate to take swift and resolute action—including the use of lightsabers when necessary.

Which two pictures do not belong to the scene?

MY FAVORITE JEDI

JEDI ACADEMIES

The Jedi Order established their academies in several locations across the galaxy to train the Force sensitives in the ways of the Force. The most famous academy was built on Coruscant, the capital of the Galactic Republic, where Master Yoda himself instructed many young Jedi adepts.

Help the Padawans find the names of these four Jedi Masters in the hologrid:

Yoda, Pong Krell, Kit Fisto, Obi-Wan

P	O	N	G	K	R	E	L	L
A	K	I	T	F	I	S	T	O
N	R	U	C	G	Y	M	Y	B
G	D	A	Y	O	D	T	U	I
K	B	Y	O	U	F	Y	J	W
R	D	Y	O	D	A	K	A	A
O	B	I	W	E	D	R	T	N

JEDI RANKS

INITIATE

The Initiates were the youngest members of the Jedi Order. Their age varied, depending on the species. They were removed from their families and brought to a Jedi academy for formal training until the Jedi Council decided they were ready for individual instruction.

PADAWAN

This rank was given to the Initiates who completed their training and were chosen by a Jedi Knight or Master for apprenticeship. Padawans were taken at adolescence and they accompanied their Masters everywhere to learn from experience and personal guidance.

KNIGHT

After nearly a decade of one-to-one training with a Master, the Padawans were eligible to attempt the Jedi Trials. If they passed all tests, they became Knights. They were no longer bound to a Master. Jedi Knights were free to travel the galaxy, accept missions from the Council, or instruct a Padawan.

MASTER

The Jedi who demonstrated the deepest understanding of the Force could be promoted by the Jedi Council to the rank of Master. Only Masters were allowed to sit on the Jedi Council. The greatest and wisest of them—the Grand Master—was the head of the Order.

LOST IN SPACE

A few young Padawans set out on a trip to the planet Tatooine. Unfortunately, the ship's central computer broke down during the flight, forcing the Jedi adepts to make use of their navigation skills. Help the unfortunate travelers find the way back to Coruscant and guide them through the maze.

YODA'S MIND TEST

Master Yoda often practices his mind skills to be stronger with the Force. Why don't you put your skills to the test? Complete the two Sudokus with numbers from 1 to 4, but make sure that the numbers don't appear twice in any row or column.

FAMOUS JEDI

YODA

The last head of the Jedi Order, Grand Master Yoda, was one of the greatest and most powerful Jedi of all. Despite his age and small size, he was an incredibly agile and dangerous swordsman, wielding a short, green-bladed lightsaber. Most Jedi in the final days of the Galactic Republic were instructed by wise Yoda.

Which piece was torn off from the picture showing Yoda fighting a giant rancor?

OBI-WAN KENOBI

Obi-Wan was a legendary Jedi who played an important role in the struggle for the freedom of the galaxy. During the invasion of Naboo, he was the first Jedi in 1,000 years to defeat a Sith Lord in combat. The Clone Wars hero and Anakin Skywalker's mentor, Obi-Wan was one of the few Jedi who survived Order 66. Later, under the name of Ben Kenobi, he trained Luke Skywalker in the ways of the Force and helped the rebels fight the Empire.

QUI-GON JINN

This wise, experienced, and sharp-witted Jedi was trained by Count Dooku (long before Dooku turned to the dark side). Perhaps this is why Qui-Gon was a maverick, who often placed himself in conflict with the Jedi Council. He was Obi-Wan Kenobi's mentor and the first to instruct a boy from Tatooine who appeared to have an incredible potential in the Force—young Anakin Skywalker.

KIT FISTO

Kit Fisto was a Nautolan Jedi Master and member of the Jedi High Council. He was an esteemed mentor to his Padawan Nahdar Vebb and a distinguished general during the Clone Wars. An expert in lightsaber combat, Kit Fisto was considered to be one of the best swordsmen in the Jedi Order. As a member of an aquatic species, he excelled in underwater combat on water worlds such as Mon Cala.

MACE WINDU

Serving on the Jedi Council, Mace Windu was considered to be second in authority only to Yoda, and his wisdom and power were as legendary as his warrior skills. He was the only practitioner of the Vaapad-style fighting technique, a combat style that he created and mastered. Windu was also the only one who wielded a lightsaber with a rare purple blade.

Which shadow belongs to Master Windu?

PONG KRELL

Pong Krell was a Besalisk who served as a general in the Republic army during the Clone Wars. This powerful Jedi was a cunning strategist who sought success on the battlefield at all costs. A recognized war hero, Pong Krell was a fierce lightsaber duelist wisely using his four arms to wield two double-bladed lightsabers simultaneously in combat.

LUMINARA UNDULI

This Mirialan Jedi Master was a respected advisor to the Jedi Council, the Supreme Chancellor, and the Galactic Senate in the fading years of the Republic. During the Clone Wars she followed the Jedi code strictly in teaching her Padawan, Barriss Offee. She was an expert practitioner of Form III and her focused, precise movements in combat impressed many fellow Jedi.

ANAKIN SKYWALKER

From slave to Jedi, Anakin's path was marked with adventures, danger, and heroic deeds. His amazing potential in the Force was discovered by Qui-Gon Jinn when Anakin was still a child. He was believed to be the Chosen One who would bring balance to the Force, and soon he became one of the most powerful Jedi of all time. But destiny wanted him to be something else . . .

HYPERSPACE MISTAKE

As the Jedi Order gathered on Coruscant to discuss plans to protect the Republic, a surprise hologram message urgently flashed into the scene. It was Chancellor Palpatine and he looked very afraid of something.

"Jedi! I NEED YOUR HELP!!!" screamed Palpatine. "They've got me!"

"Who has you, Chancellor?" asked Mace Windu, Master of the Jedi Order.

"I have him!" an evil voice cackled as General Grievous nudged into the hologram. "So na-nanny boo-boo, you Jedi goody two-shoes!"

"Ugh, Chancellor, really? You were captured by this guy?" asked Kit Fisto.

"Yes, well, I can hardly believe it myself," mumbled Palpatine. "Anyway, Grievous is holding me hostage, but he doesn't know about my homing beacon belt. Here are my coordinates . . . now, come and help me—before it's too late!"

"Okay, Jedi, you heard the Chancellor," called out Mace Windu. "Who's coming with me to save Palpatine and knock some sense into those Separatists?"

The members of the Jedi Order all raised their hands to volunteer.

Just then the hologram flickered back on. It was the Chancellor again. "One last thing I forgot to mention. If at all possible, could you leave Yoda behind? We really should have one Jedi around to watch the shop, you know?"

"*Hmmmm.* Nice, a little me time would be," said Yoda approvingly.

"Excellent!" Palpatine smiled. "So it's agreed. Yoda stays and the rest of the Order shall come to meet their total doom, um, I mean, to save me from total doom. Thanks and peace out!"

Immediately, a fleet of Jedi starfighters left Coruscant and blasted toward the Chancellor's tracking signal. Mace and Kit led the way aboard the same ship.

"Mace, did it strike you as odd that Grievous let Palpatine give us so much information about where he is being held hostage?" asked Kit.

"It bothered me until I realized that we're talking about General Grievous," laughed Mace. "That cyborg just isn't put together the right way."

The two Jedi shared a laugh and zipped through space. Little did they know that they were racing toward a terrible trap.

As soon as the Jedi pulled out of lightspeed, an armada of enemy ships was waiting for them. A barrage of blasts shot at the Jedi starfighters, but they swiftly navigated the attacks and fired back.

Obi-Wan Kenobi rammed one ship with his starfighter, knocking it into a second, third, and fourth ship, but instead of exploding, all the ships wings locked together to create an even bigger ship.

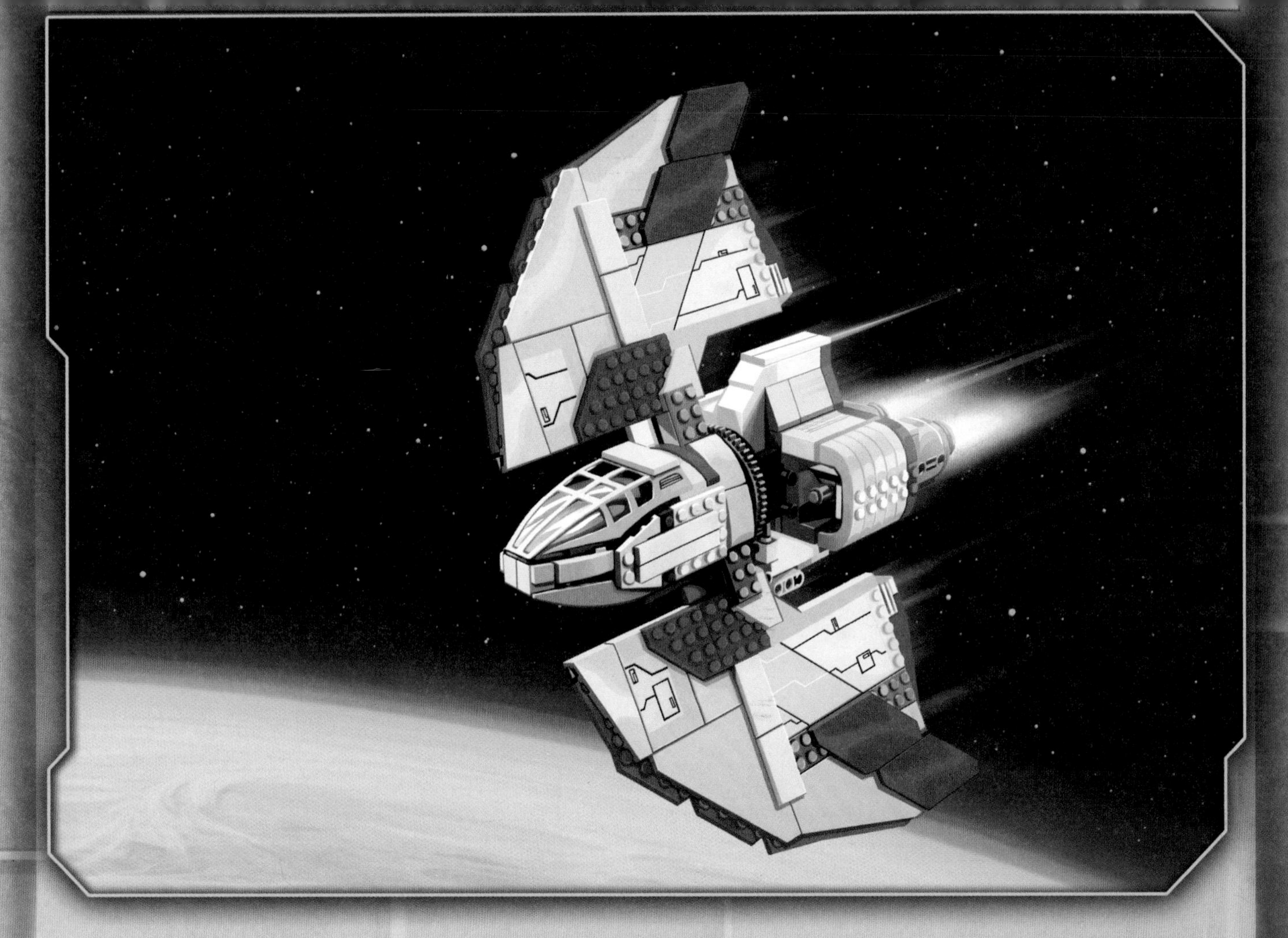

“Well, that was unexpected,” said Obi-Wan as the new large ship turned toward him. Luckily, Ki-Adi-Mundi flew in with a mighty blast that destroyed the large ship in a domino effect of explosions.

After the battlefield cleared, only General Grievous’s shuttle remained.

Using the Force, Kit held the shuttle in place while Mace Force lifted the Chancellor out of the evil grip of Grievous and into their spaceship.

“Oh, great, I’m saved,” said Palpatine snidely. “I really thought this clone armada would annihilate you and your Order.”

“No way, sir,” said Kit. “It would take a lot more than those puny punks to beat us. Now, let’s get that faulty-parts-cyborg and head home.”

“Of course, Jedi,” Palpatine smiled. “Do your best.” Then, just as Kit and Mace turned their attention to General Grievous, the evil Chancellor Palpatine thrust the ship into hyperdrive! “Oh, clumsy me, look what I’ve done.”

The starship zoomed into hyperspace as the control board blared in alarm. Mace and Kit ran to manage the situation. As they tried to plot the ship’s path, it didn’t look good. “Sir, I really wish you hadn’t done that,” said Mace. “You see a ship launched into hyperspace without a clear destination could crash into anything along the way . . . another spaceship, an asteroid, even a . . . ”

“Mace, it looks like we’re heading straight to Naboo!” said Kit.

“Naboo? I hear it’s lovely there this time of year.” Palpatine smiled.

“It is . . . until we crash into it and fracture its core!” hollered Mace as Kit tried to undo whatever the Chancellor had done to their controls.

“*Hmmm*, and that would be a very bad thing for two top Jedi to do, wouldn’t it?” said Palpatine as he inched toward the door to escape. “I know that if you destroyed Naboo under my watch, I’d have to do away with the entire Jedi Order. You’d be a hazard to the safety and well-being of the Republic . . . which would make you public enemy number one! And now my masterful plan is about to come—”

But before Palpatine could finish his thought, the starfighter lurched to a halt, tossing Mace and Kit against the Chancellor, who was pinned against a window. The ship hovered only a few feet above the ground on Naboo, and underneath it was none other than Yoda. He had stopped the ship using the Force!

“Oh, no-da. Not Yoda,” said Chancellor Palpatine as he slid slowly down the windshield.

“*Hmmm*. Very lucky, you are,” said Yoda. “Nice here, this time of year it is, so visit and see the sights, I did. But to the Jedi, leave the driving from now on, Chancellor. And remember: Always buckle up. For a bumpy ride, it could be.”

LIGHTSABERS

For thousands of years the lightsaber was the symbol of the Jedi, the righteous protectors of the galactic peace. It was an elegant weapon, not as crude as a blaster, and certainly not as popular. To carry a lightsaber was an example of remarkable skill and ability to use the Force. The lengths of the hilt and blade, as well as the blade's color, varied greatly because the Jedi constructed their individual weapons to suit their own specific needs. The typical lightsaber consisted of a metal hilt that emitted a blade of pure plasma that could cut through almost anything and deflect even laser bolts.

QUICK QUIZ

?! Q

The lightsabers used by the Jedi were all the same size. True or false?

JEDI SOCCER

The Jedi must always be in perfect shape. That is why sports are an important part of the Jedi training. The young Padawans play all kinds of games, but sometimes it's not easy to follow their rules . . .

LIGHTSABER COMBAT FORMS

Using the experience gained over the millennia by their best swordsmen, the Jedi academies trained the Jedi adepts in seven forms of Jedi lightsaber combat. The forms were developed for different purposes and varied in difficulty.

FORM I: SHII-CHO

It's the foundation upon which the remaining forms build. It consists of basic moves that must be mastered and repeated quickly and fluidly. Practicing with a training remote is the first step in learning Form I. The younglings who start with Form I use training lightsabers.

FORM II: MAKASHI

This is the most elegant of all lightsaber forms and it is the best style for lightsaber-to-lightsaber dueling. Makashi emphasizes precision strikes and well-balanced footwork. It is a one-handed style, therefore its users prefer well-balanced lightsabers, including curved-hilt variants.

FORM III: SORESU

Soresu is a defensive technique, which is ideal for intercepting blaster fire. It involves predicting the incoming multiple laser bolts and deflecting them aside with quick, short movements. Practitioners of Form III (Obi-Wan, for instance) claimed it often kept them alive when they stumbled into an ambush.

FORM IV: ATARU

Ataru emphasizes acrobatic abilities and incredibly quick jumps and lunges. Form IV requires excellent lightsaber skills, and its exhausting style is best practiced by Jedi who can easily enhance their speed and stamina through the Force. Despite his age, Yoda was a true master of Ataru.

FORM V: SHIEN

Form V requires less agility or finesse than other forms, because it focuses mainly on the Jedi's physical strength to withstand the heavy blaster fire, deflect it toward the attacker, and counterstrike immediately with violent blows. It is the most physically demanding of all combat styles.

FORM VI: NIMAN

Niman draws from all styles and encourages integrating Force powers into combat. The telekinetic pulls and shoves combined with fairly relaxed lightsaber strikes allowed the Jedi to take control of a group of enemies and eliminate them one by one. Form VI was the Jedi Consulars' favorite combat style.

FORM VII: JUYO (VAAPAD)

Named after a predatory creature from the world of Sarapin, the style was developed by Mace Windu. It was characterized by quick and deadly strikes to overcome the enemy. This offensive style required full control of its practitioners' violent instincts, otherwise it could lead them straight to the dark side.

CLONE TROOPERS

Clone troopers were an army of identical, genetically modified soldiers created in the cloning facilities on Kamino to serve in the Grand Army of the Republic. Using the genetic material of a bounty hunter named Jango Fett, the Kaminoans bred and trained thousands of clones for one purpose only—military combat. As a result, the clone troopers were utterly disciplined soldiers who obeyed orders from their commanders without question.

Under the command of the Jedi generals the clone army became one of the most efficient military forces in the history of the galaxy. Engaged in battles on many fronts, the Jedi failed to see that the clones were a big part of the Sith plan to take control of the galaxy.

LOGICAL SOLUTION

Master Obi-Wan has a task for you. The colorful symbols in the three rows are placed in a specific order. What colors will end each sequence? Write the correct letters in the empty spaces.

THE CLONE WARS

The Clone Wars were a major galactic conflict between the Republic and the Confederacy of Independent Systems. The war earned its name after the clone troopers used by the Republic against the Separatists' battle droids. After the first battle on Geonosis, the opposing armies clashed repeatedly over the next three years, spreading the war across the galaxy to countless inhabited worlds.

Write the letters in the correct boxes to learn the names of the Separatist leader and the cyborg-general who commanded his droid army.

JEDI STAR FLEET

REPUBLIC STARFIGHTER

These small, multipurpose *Striker*-class starfighters were very popular among the Jedi pilots in the days of the Old Republic. During the Great Galactic War they served as the primary defense against the Sith interceptors, but they were also used for escorting diplomatic convoys or short-range reconnaissance missions. Like many small ships of that time, the *Striker*-class fighters did not have hyperdrive engines, so larger ships carried them to distant destinations. However, an astromech droid that helped the pilot navigate was standard equipment.

QUICK QUIZ

?!Q

The *Striker*-class fighters were mostly used for deep-space reconnaissance missions. True or false?

THE ALLIES OF THE REPUBLIC

WOOKIEES

The Wookiees were the inhabitants of the jungle world of Kashyyyk. They lived in tree houses and from an early age learned to carve tools and simple devices out of wood. While they appeared to have a low technology level to outsiders, the Wookiees were in fact quite comfortable with modern technology. They were renowned for their great strength, intelligence, and loyalty. Despite their fearsome appearance they were usually gentle, although they were known to lose their temper and rage in anger if provoked.

QUICK QUIZ

?! Q

The Wookiees are by nature an extremely loyal species. True or false?

GUNGANS

The Gungans were intelligent, amphibious inhabitants of Naboo. Those peaceful creatures preferred to stay away from surface-dwelling Naboo and lived in large bubble-like domes under water. Their unique technology allowed them to travel through the planet's core or shield their constructions with an energy field (which proved to be very useful during the invasion of the Trade Federation army on Naboo).

EWOKS

These small, furry beings lived on the forest moon of Endor. They were very friendly, extremely curious, and resourceful. When they learned that the Imperial forces were a threat to their existence, they agreed to help the rebels fight them. The brave Ewoks turned out to be cunning warriors without whom the rebels would not have been able to destroy the shield generator protecting the second Death Star.

JEDI QUIZ

Are you ready for a short memory test? Choose one answer to each question in this quiz and find out what you remember about the Jedi and their world. Try not to look back at the pages of the book until you're done. May the Force be with you.

1. Which organization protected the peace in the galaxy?
   a. The Jedi Order
   b. Trade Federation
   c. The Sith Order

2. What does a being's potential in the Force depend on?
   a. Intelligence and physical strength
   b. Reading, writing, and counting skills
   c. The midi-chlorian count in the blood cells

3. Which aspect of the Force is dedicated to harmony and peace?
   a. The light side of the Force
   b. The colorful side of the Force
   c. The dark side of the Force

4. What planet was the most famous Jedi Academy located on?
   a. Naboo
   b. Geonosis
   c. Coruscant

5. What was the color of Yoda's lightsaber?
   a. Red
   b. Purple
   c. Green

6. Which Jedi found a boy who was thought to be the Chosen One?
   a. Obi-Wan Kenobi
   b. Qui-Gon Jinn
   c. Mace Windu

7. How many lightsaber combat forms were practiced by the Jedi?
   a. 8
   b. 7
   c. 5

8. What battle started the Clone Wars?
   a. The Battle of Geonosis
   b. The Battle of Endor
   c. The Battle of Naboo

9. Whose genetic material was used to create the Republic clone troopers?
   a. Anakin Skywalker's
   b. Kit Fisto's
   c. Jango Fett's

10. What species inhabited the forest moon of Endor?
   a. The Gungans
   b. The Ewoks
   c. The Wookiees

ANSWERS

Quick Quiz
Pg. 2: False
Pg. 18: False
Pg. 25: False
Pg. 26: True

Pg. 4 The Jedi Order
Pictures 2 and 4.

Pg. 6 Jedi Academies

P	O	N	G	K	R	E	L	L
A	K	I	T	F	I	S	T	O
N	R	U	C	G	Y	M	Y	B
G	D	A	Y	O	D	T	U	I
K	B	Y	O	U	F	Y	J	W
R	D	Y	O	D	A	K	A	A
O	B	I	W	E	D	R	T	N

Pg. 8 Lost in Space

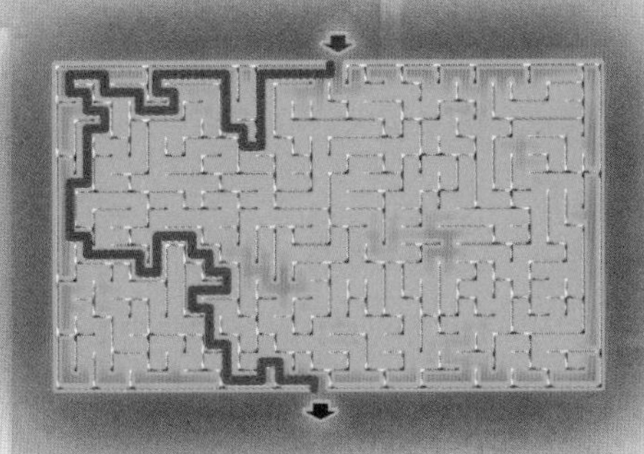

Pg. 9 Yoda's Mind Test

A

B

Pg. 10 Famous Jedi
Picture 2.

Pg. 12 Mace Windu
Shadow 3.

Pg. 23 Logical Solution
1 – B
2 – C
3 – A

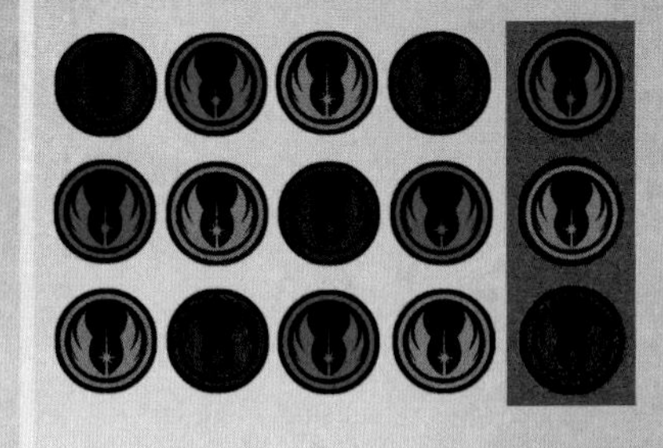

Pg. 24 Clone Wars
DOOKU
GRIEVOUS

Pgs. 30–31 Jedi Quiz
1 – a, 2 – c, 3 – a, 4 – c, 5 – c,
6 – b, 7 – b, 8 – a, 9 – c, 10 – b.

THE POWER OF THE SITH....

Peaceful days never last long in the universe. The continuing clashes between the followers of the light and the dark sides of the Force ended with victories on both sides. The unwavering Jedi Knights stood on guard for galactic peace, while their archenemies—the Order of the Sith—reached out for total control over the galaxy again and again. The Sith Lords pursued power at all costs. Over the millennia, they cultivated greed, anger and hatred in their hearts, and recruited new powerful followers. Eventually, using deceit and manipulation, they achieved their goal and led to the fall of the Republic. The rule of the evil Galactic Empire began . . .

SITH LORDS

Some powerful Sith Lords were the Jedi who had turned to the dark side of the Force. Those fallen Jedi renounced the path of virtue, justice, and selflessness in order to gain more power that they could use for their own benefit. As they started a new life as the Sith, they called themselves "Darths" and took new names, like Darth Sidious or Darth Vader.

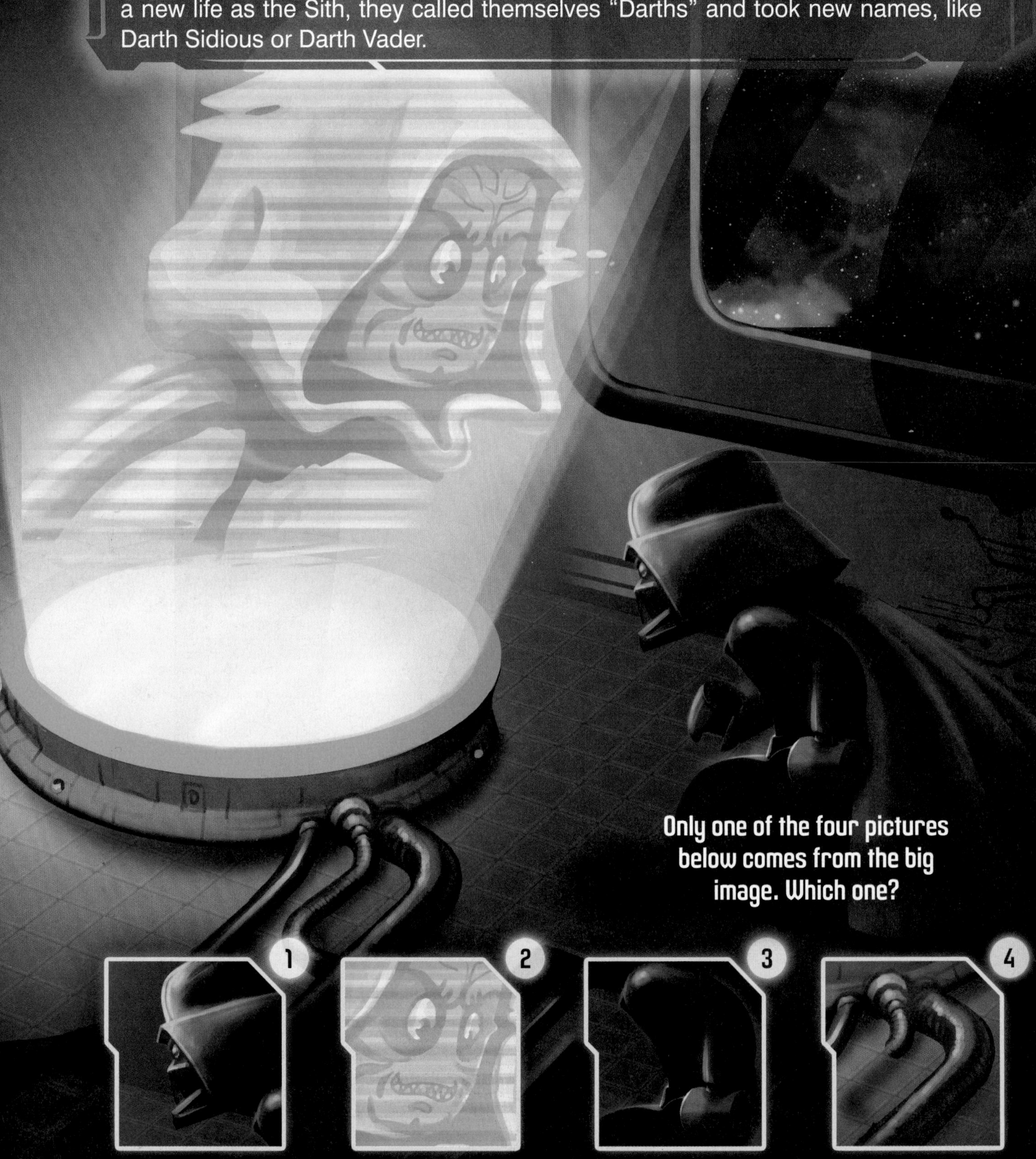

Only one of the four pictures below comes from the big image. Which one?

THE FALLEN JEDI

Even the greatest members of the Jedi Order could not resist the power of the dark side. Count Dooku was one of the most renowned swordsmen in the galaxy and a respected teacher in the Jedi Temple (he was Qui-Gon Jinn's first instructor). Despite being a Jedi for nearly seventy years, Dooku was suddenly lured by the power of the Sith. He became Darth Sidious's apprentice known as Darth Tyranus.

QUICK QUIZ

?! Q

Dooku had been a Dark Lord of the Sith for seventy years before turning to the light side. True or false?

THE DARK PATH

Like all users of the Force, the Sith Lords had amazing abilities that gave them an advantage over other beings. Striving for more power, they followed the dark side of the Force for quicker and better results. However, it was the dark side that controlled the Sith, corrupted them, and made them utterly evil.

Put the missing fragments in the correct places in the picture.

DARK RITUALS

Throughout the years, the Sith developed many dark rituals that served one purpose—to intimidate their enemies. Many Sith hid their faces behind masks and wore dark cloaks to look frightening. Others—like the Zabrak species—applied scary tattoos on their faces or even entire bodies.

Follow the lines and put the letters in the boxes to read the name of the dark side warrior fighting the two Jedi.

DARK SIDE POWERS

The wielders of the dark side of the Force did not hesitate to use their powers in the cruelest ways. The Sith were able to move large and heavy objects without touching them and throw them like missiles at their opponents. Some would often Force choke people to punish them, or prove their strength to others. The most powerful Sith, like Darth Sidious, could even unleash lethal storms of lightning from their palms.

QUICK QUIZ

Darth Sidious could attack enemies with a powerful Force lightning. True or false?

DARTH MAUL

Darth Maul was a Zabrak Sith Lord from planet Dathomir. Trained by Darth Sidious in the ways of the dark side, he quickly became a skilled warrior who completed many secret missions for his evil master. During a mission on Naboo, Maul was defeated by a young Jedi Padawan named Obi-Wan Kenobi. Maul was thought to be dead, but he had survived, and many years later he returned, walking on mechanical legs to serve the dark side of the Force.

Which of the three faces is the face of Darth Maul?

1

2

3

VADER'S MISSION

Darth Sidious has sent his new apprentice, Darth Vader, on a secret mission. Vader is known for his unmatched skills in lightsaber combat. Whomever gets in the Dark Lord's way is doomed. Will you accept Vader's challenge?

This picture was cut into pieces, and they all got mixed up. One piece was accidentally replaced by a wrong one. Can you spot the wrong piece?

HOW TO BE A SITH

NOW, MY APPRENTICE, I'LL TELL YOU HOW TO BE A REAL SITH. LET'S START WITH THE LOOK. YOUR LOOK MUST SHROUD EVERYTHING IN DARKNESS!
UM . . . DARKNESS . . .

AS FOR THE COLORS OF YOUR CLOTHES, THERE ARE MANY OPTIONS. GLOSSY BLACK, MATTE BLACK, PITCH BLACK, COAL BLACK, OR— IF YOU'RE VERY PICKY—EERIE BLACK.
UM . . . BLACK . . .

THE SITH MAY KEEP PETS. THE TUK'ATA ARE COOL, BUT YOU HAVE TO WALK THEM AT LEAST TWICE A DAY, WHICH CAN BE QUITE INCONVENIENT DURING LONG SPACE JOURNEYS. IF YOU GET ONE, IT BETTER BE VERY, VERY DARK!
UM . . . VERY DARK . . .

THE REAL SITH EAT BLACK SAUSAGE AND BLACK OLIVES. AND THEY DRINK COFFEE—BLACK!

BUT, YOU KNOW, SOMETIMES EVEN I AM TEMPTED BY THE LIGHT SIDE OF THE FORCE AND I DREAM OF SWEET CREAM PUDDING . . .
???

SITH STARSHIPS

SITH INFILTRATOR

The *Infiltrator* was one of a kind. This prototype stealth ship was built at Republic Sienar Systems' secret facilities that specialized in experimental technologies and unique designs. The *Infiltrator* was a heavily modified and armed Star Courier—a fast ship intended for delivery of urgent cargo and very important passengers.

The sleek elongated front part of the ship's hull contained a large cargo hold where a small reconnaissance speeder bike and several probe droids could be loaded. The upper deck of the spherical cockpit had seats for the pilot and six passengers, while the lower deck was divided into four storage bays and two small sleeping compartments. Besides the pilot, the crew consisted of several interrogation and security droids. The ship was equipped with a cloaking device for creating an invisibility field. This enabled the ship to sneak through even the most advanced of security technologies and easily evade pursuit. Numerous sensors, tracking devices, and advanced navigation system made space travel fast and easy for the pilot.

Darth Maul flew the *Infiltrator* on many dangerous missions, including when he had to track down the missing Queen Amidala. This was Maul's last mission using the ship before he was wounded in a fight with Amidala's Jedi protectors on Naboo.

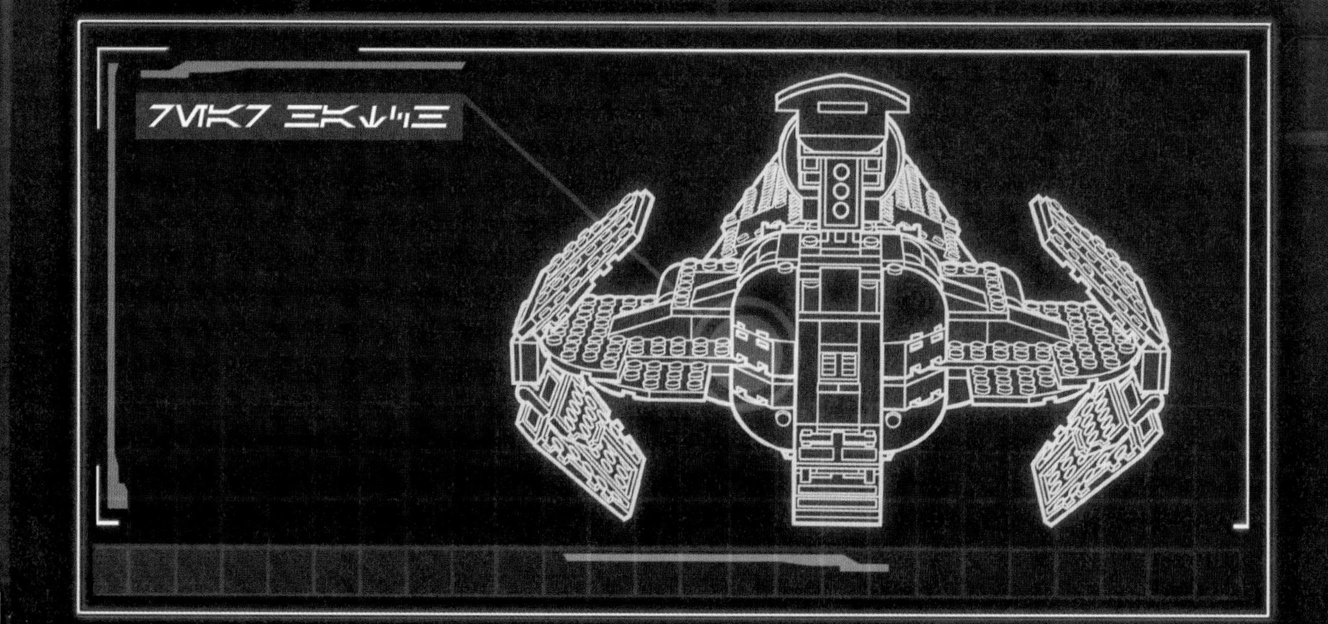

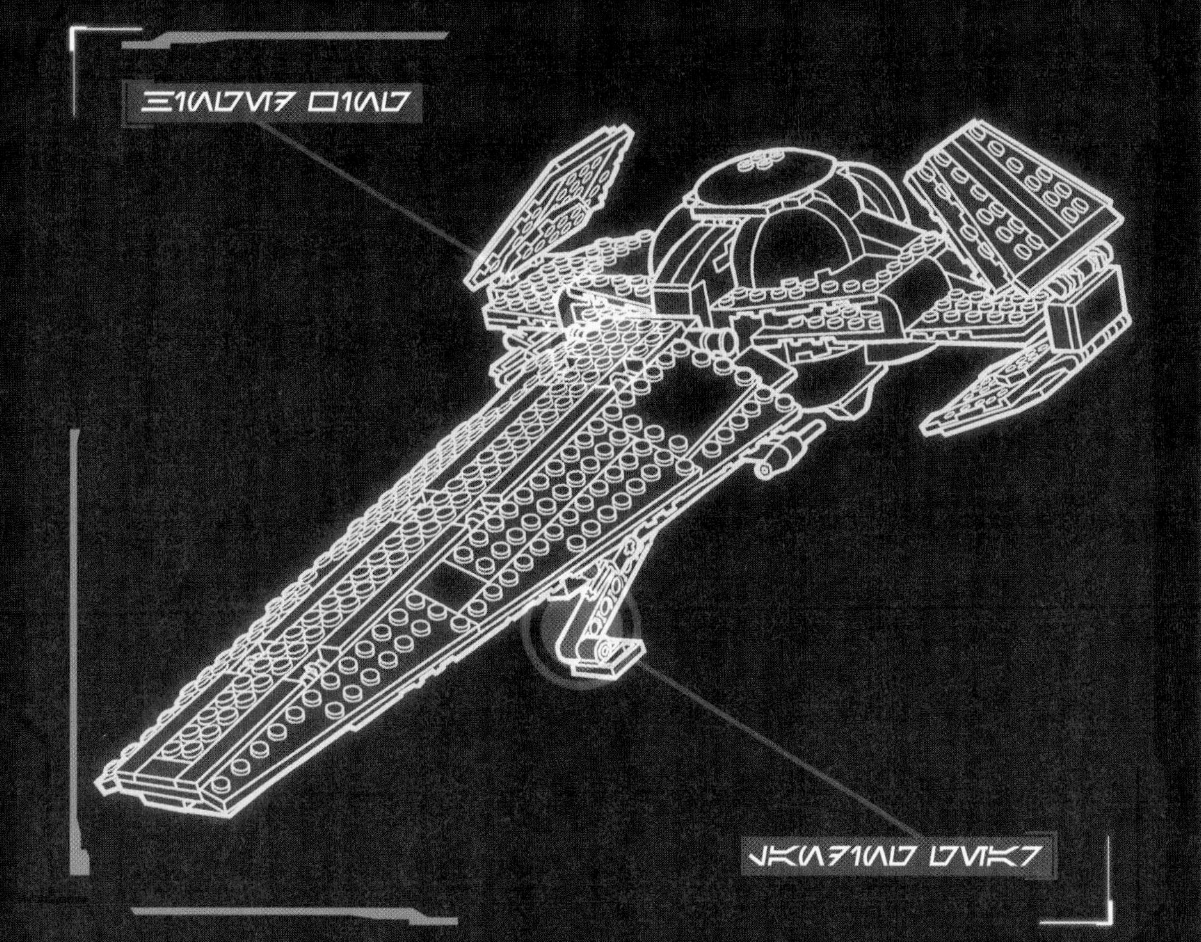

TECHNICAL DETAILS

LENGTH: 265 m
MAXIMUM SPEED (in atmosphere): 730 mph
CARGO CAPACITY: 5,000 lbs
WEAPONS: 6 concealed solar ionization cannons
SPECIAL FEATURES: Stygium cloaking device

DATA FILE

CLASS: Space transport
MANUFACTURER: Republic Sienar Systems
COST: 55,000,000 credits

THE DARKEST SIDE WINS

Gazing at a map of the Empire's total conquests stretching across the galaxy, the Emperor sat back in his chair and sighed. The leader of the Galactic Empire was not happy.

"Vader! Maul!" beckoned the Emperor. His faithful Sith Lords pushed and shoved past each other into the room. "There's still not enough evil out there. Sure, we've done a decent job of spreading the dark side, but there's *hope* growing. It's hiding somewhere on this map. And we need to crush it."

Darth Maul slashed the map in half with his lightsaber. "Did I get it?"

The Emperor's hands flared up and shocked Maul with Force lightning. "You redheaded thorn brain!" he scolded. "There is hope in the galaxy, not the map. So I want you two hammerheads to go do your worst in the most hopeful corners of this galaxy."

"Ugh, not with him!" Vader and Maul whined, looking at each other reluctantly.

"*Enough!*" shouted the Emperor. "Make sure everyone knows that there will be *no hope* under my command. And let's make it a contest. Whoever wreaks the most havoc will be my right-hand man . . . er, sorry, Vader, you know what I mean."

The Sith Lords grumbled as they boarded their spaceships and blasted off in different directions.

Vader shifted into hyperspace toward a small moon known as Endor where a tribe of hopeful beings known as Ewoks lived. Vader detested those happy little Ewoks . . . almost as much as he detested Darth Maul.

Flying over the forest, Vader's sensors picked up an awful racket: singing.

Below him, a group of short fuzzy creatures were dancing and singing around a bonfire. They raised their spears in the air as fireworks exploded brightly in the sky.

"A celebration?" questioned Vader. "I'll give them something to celebrate . . . the impending doom of the Empire!"

Leaping from his ship, Vader landed in the fire and sent every last Ewok scrambling away in fear. "Good! I find your lack of hope delightful!"

Satisfied by his total domination of the Ewok tribe, Vader returned to his ship and contacted Maul to brag about his victory.

"Wow, so you scared away a bunch of cute little teddy-weddy bears?" scoffed Maul. "A protocol droid could easily do that! Look what I've caught for the Emperor!"

Maul's hologram pulled back to reveal a giant cage filled with rebel Wookiees baring their teeth and screaming at the top of their lungs.

"Advantage goes to me!" Maul laughed.

Vader didn't stick around to hear Maul's bragging. His radar detected a fleet of rebel ships flying in a restricted area. Cloaked in darkness, he snuck in behind the ships and launched a surprise attack. The rebels had no time to defend themselves as Vader swept through space and blasted each ship one by one. By the time the battle was over, Vader had captured the entire fleet and Force built a prison ship to jail the rebel pilots.

Maul's hologram popped back up with his gnarled grin. "Hey, chrome dome, guess who just caught a rebel spaceship?"

"Hey, horn-head, guess who just caught an entire rebel fleet?" Vader laughed. "Now we're even."

Maul screamed in frustration and ended the call. Suddenly, Vader felt a very strong disturbance in the Force coming from Naboo. It was the biggest sense of hope he had ever felt, so he bolted to the planet right away.

When he arrived in Theed, Vader found a small hooded old man with a cane carrying a wooden box. This man was a source of vast hope, but Vader didn't know why.

As Vader struggled to solve the mystery, Darth Maul appeared as if from nowhere and surprise-attacked the old man. He sliced through the box first, spilling red berries everywhere. The man evaded Maul's second strike and pulled back his hood to reveal a pair of long green ears and a shock of white hair. It was Yoda!

"Found on my planet, Muja fruit is not. A special trip to Naboo, I made. Fighting, I hadn't planned on. But fight, I will."

Maul charged forward again, but Yoda quickly waved his hand and Force tied the cyborg-Sith's mechanical legs together. Maul crashed to the ground and landed face first in the smashed Muja berries.

Yoda turned to see Vader already coming right at him with an ignited red lightsaber. A green blade flashed in the Jedi Master's hand and a fierce battle erupted. Sparks flew as the lightsabers clashed with parrying and thrusting strikes in a

blur of motion. The duel was brutal and swift until finally Yoda Force pushed his opponent against a brick wall. The wall collapsed and Vader disappeared under the debris.

"Disturb a Jedi while shopping, you must never. Very rude, it is," Yoda said and switched off his lightsaber. "Lesson learned, I hope."

"Hope! There won't be any hope in the galaxy! Not on my watch!" shouted Vader, suddenly emerging from underneath the debris. In a flash, he Force built a spaceship around Yoda from the discarded bricks and blasted the very surprised Jedi Master deep into space.

"Where'd you send him?" asked Maul as he crawled over.

"To a galaxy far, far away, Darth Muja-berry-face." Vader laughed. "And that means the winner is me!"

"You fool! We had Yoda trapped, and you let him go!" screamed Maul. "What are we going to tell the Emperor?!"

Vader paused and considered what he'd just done. "*Hmmm*, how about we call it a dark side draw and the Emperor never has to hear about this . . . unfortunate incident?"

And for once, the Sith rivals were in complete agreement.

THE RULE OF TWO

Although at one time there were many Sith, they were not able to defeat the Jedi and take control of the galaxy. Then Darth Bane created the Rule of Two. He believed that the Sith Order should be a secret organization consisting of a Sith master and an apprentice. This way, the Force would fuel its great power into two beings at a time, making them super-powerful.

Find the names of these two Sith Lords—Sidious and Maul—in the grid. The names can be written down or across.

S	E	R	W	O	L	G	U
G	I	G	J	A	Y	G	M
I	S	D	M	A	M	W	A
K	D	Y	I	K	A	S	U
S	I	D	I	O	U	S	O
M	S	I	D	I	L	O	K
I	G	S	C	M	A	U	R
D	U	O	S	I	D	I	U

SECRET WEAPON

The path to the ultimate domination in the galaxy was a long one. Darth Sidious and his apprentice, Darth Tyranus, were always thinking ahead. As their plan to disrupt the peace in the galaxy was turning into reality, the Sith secretly launched a new project: the building of a moon-sized space battle station. The Death Star, as they called it, would have enough firepower to destroy an entire planet . . .

QUICK QUIZ

The new weapon of the Sith could blow up a planet into pieces with a single laser blast. True or false?

ORDER 66

It was a big surprise for the Jedi to learn that one of them, Master Sifo-Dyas, had ordered the creation of an army of clones for the Republic. The clone troopers were bred and trained to obey orders without question. During the Clone Wars, they fought under the Jedi generals, but when Chancellor Palpatine issued Order 66, they obeyed it and opened fire at their generals. It was the end of the Jedi Order.

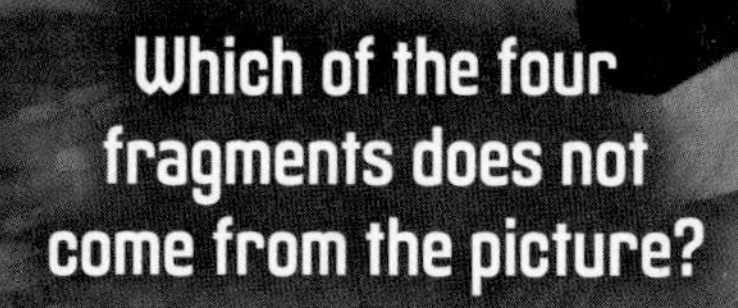

A

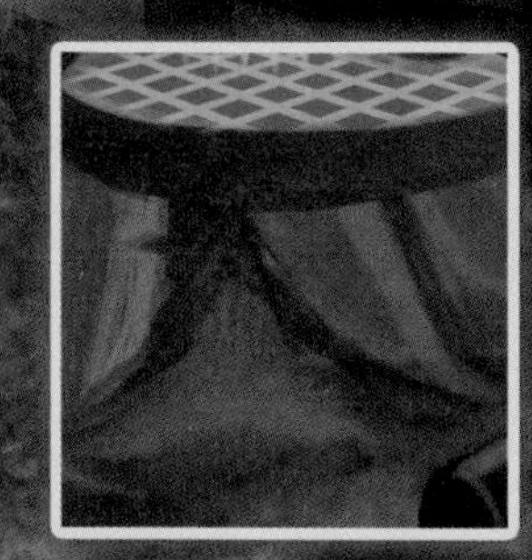

B

C

D

DARTH SIDIOUS

Everyone in the Old Republic knew him as friendly Senator Palpatine from Naboo. Neither the other Senators nor the Jedi suspected that Palpatine was a Sith Lord in disguise. Darth Sidious—as he called himself—had plotted a wicked scheme to gain the ultimate power in the galaxy. He became the Supreme Chancellor of the Galactic Republic only to bring disorder to the Republic with the help from his two succeeding apprentices, Darth Maul and Darth Tyranus.

QUICK QUIZ

?! Q

Chancellor Palpatine was a Dark Lord of the Sith in disguise. True or false?

THE GALACTIC EMPIRE

The years of plotting and scheming finally brought the long-awaited results. With one swift move, Palpatine, or rather Darth Sidious, had destroyed his greatest enemies, the Jedi. He immediately announced the fall of the Republic and the beginning of the First Galactic Empire. He made himself the Emperor, while his new apprentice—Darth Vader—became his right-hand man.

Which lightsaber hilt is the same as the one in Vader's hand?

IMPERIAL ARMY

When the Clone Wars ended and the reign of the Sith began, the Republic's Grand Army was reformed into the Imperial Army. Unconditionally loyal to the Emperor, the clones—renamed as "stormtroopers"—quickly built a reputation of merciless enforcers of the New Order.

Can you spot 5 small differences between the two pictures?

THE EMPEROR

During the first years of its existence, the Empire developed its military power. With the great army at his orders, the Emperor took over new planets, where he established imperial governors and stormtrooper garrisons. Imperial agents hunted the surviving Jedi and tracked down sources of resistance against the Empire. Sidious gradually tightened his grip on the galaxy.

DARTH VADER

The Emperor could not have asked for a better enforcer of the Imperial rule than Vader. His loyal apprentice was a fallen Jedi, a powerful user of the Force, and one of the most fearsome warriors in the galaxy. In the service of his evil Sith master, Darth Vader spread terror to every corner of his new Empire.

Which of these three pictures is a mirror reflection of the big image?

HAPPY BIRTHDAY, MASTER!

OUCH!
YOU DESTROYED MY BIRTHDAY CAKE!

YOU ATTACKED ME AND TRIED TO TAKE MY PLACE!

YOU ARE BAD! BAD TO THE BONE, VADER!

I HAVE NEVER HOPED FOR A BETTER BIRTHDAY GIFT, MY BOY!

THE PROPHECY

In the last years of the Republic, the Jedi remembered an old prophecy about a hero who would bring balance to the Force. Master Qui-Gon Jinn believed that the prophecy referred to a Force-sensitive boy named Anakin Skywalker, whom he had found on the remote planet Tatooine. In time, the boy became an incredibly powerful Jedi. But fate played a cruel joke on the Jedi Order when Anakin turned to the dark side and became Darth Vader.

Write the numbers of the elements in the correct places to complete the picture.

SPACE PURSUIT

During a scouting mission, a rebel X-wing pilot spotted a lonely TIE fighter flying in space. It was Darth Vader's fighter! The rebel can't miss the opportunity to catch the leader of the Empire. Guide the X-wing through the maze, so it can follow the Imperial fighter.

FATHER AND SON

Many years after his transformation into a Sith Lord, Vader met his son, Luke Skywalker. Following the Emperor's instructions, he tried to turn Luke to the dark side. He lured him with a vision of overthrowing the Emperor and ruling the galaxy together. Although father and son crossed their lightsabers, something started to change in Vader's heart . . .

QUICK QUIZ

?!

Luke Skywalker was Anakin Skywalker's younger brother. True or false?

THE CHOSEN ONE

Anakin Skywalker was supposed to be the Chosen One, but instead of bringing balance to the Force, he inspired fear and caused destruction as Darth Vader. However, under his son's influence, Vader discovered that there was still some good in him. He sacrificed his own life to save Luke and destroy the Emperor. His selfless act ended the terror of the Sith. It took a long time before the Jedi prophecy was finally fulfilled.

Which of these three elements comes from the big picture?

1

2

3

BATTLE AMONG THE STARS

The Sith tried many times to take control of the galaxy. They sent their powerful star fleet to defeat the Republic, but the Jedi fleet was always prepared to fight the Sith off.
Look carefully at the two pictures. They should be identical, but the space battle scene below is missing a few elements. See if you can spot them.

SITH QUIZ

If you think that you know everything about the Sith, you are mistaken. There are still a lot of secrets left for you to reveal. But now test your memory and try to answer every question in this quiz.

1. What title did the Sith Lords usually place before their names?
   a. Duke
   b. Count
   c. Darth

2. Who was Count Dooku's apprentice, when he was still a Jedi?
   a. Luke Skywalker
   b. Obi-Wan Kenobi
   c. Qui-Gon Jinn

3. What was Darth Maul's homeworld?
   a. Tatooine
   b. Dathomir
   c. Naboo

4. What did the Sith call their new super-powerful battle station?
   a. Death Star
   b. Dark Star
   c. Sith Star

5. Who issued the fatal Order 66?
   a. Jedi Generals
   b. Chancellor Palpatine
   c. Anakin Skywalker

6. Who introduced the Rule of Two?
   a. Darth Tyranus
   b. Darth Bane
   c. Darth Sidious

7. What did the Sith Lords do to inspire fear in their opponents?
   a. They wore scary tattoos.
   b. They screamed loud during battles.
   c. They sang scary songs before battle.

8. What was the greatest achievement of Darth Sidious?
   a. He destroyed the Jedi Order and created the First Galactic Empire.
   b. He turned Luke Skywalker to the dark side.
   c. He destroyed the Sith and their Galactic Empire.

9. Who was the Chosen One from the Jedi prophecy?
   a. Chancellor Palpatine
   b. Anakin Skywalker
   c. Qui-Gon Jinn

10. What name did Anakin Skywalker take when he turned to the dark side?
    a. Maul
    b. Vader
    c. Luke

ANSWERS

Quick Quiz
Pg. 33: False
Pg. 48: True
Pg. 50: True
Pg. 60: False

Pg. 32 Sith Lords
Picture 2.

Pg. 34 The Dark Path

Pg. 35 Dark Rituals
SAVAGE OPRESS

Pg. 37 Darth Maul
Face 3.

Pg. 38 Vader's Mission
Piece 2.

Pg. 47 The Rule of Two

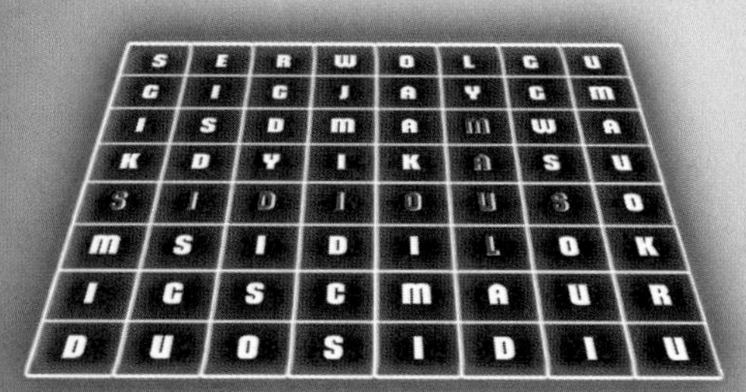

Pg. 49 Order 66
Fragment C.

Pg. 51 The Galactic Empire
Hilt B.

Pgs. 52–53 Imperial Army

Pg. 54 The Emperor
Brick C.

Pg. 55 Darth Vader
Picture 2.

Pg. 58 The Prophecy

Pg. 59 Space Pursuit

Pg. 61 The Chosen One
Piece 1.

Pg. 62 Battle Among the Stars

Pgs. 64–65 Sith Quiz
1 – c, 2 – c, 3 – b,
4 – a, 5 – b, 6 – b,
7 – a, 8 – a, 9 – b,
10 – b.

GALACTIC FREEDOM FIGHTERS...

As the Galactic Civil War raged on, new legions of brave rebel fighters joined the Rebel Alliance every day . . . perhaps only to impress the beautiful Princess Leia.

THE REBEL ARMY

The Rebel Alliance was a united group of underground heroes fighting to defeat the evil Galactic Empire. The Sith Lord Darth Vader and his stormtroopers constantly hunted for these "rebels" throughout the galaxy.

Which one of these scenes doesn't fit in the picture below?

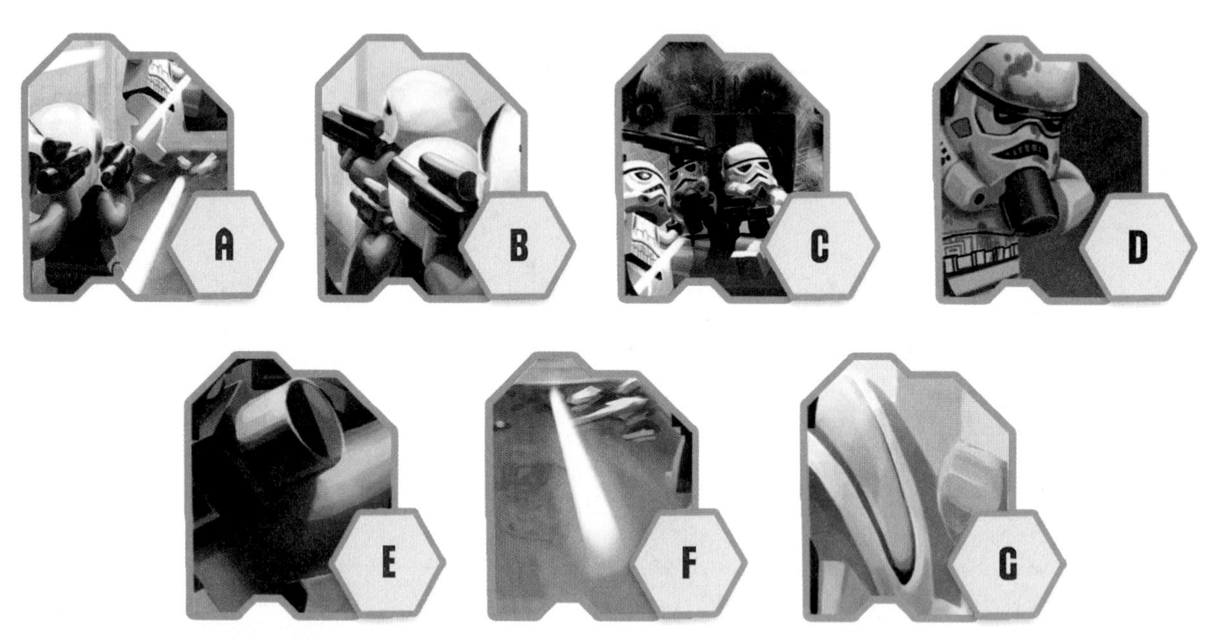

ROGUE SQUADRON

This legendary rebel starfighter armada was known for blasting off into the most extreme missions on their X-wings. Erase every second letter in the frames and find out the name of the most famous Rogue Squadron pilot.

WSETDJGKE

ABNXTZIPLHLYERS

_ _ _ _ _   _ _ _ _ _ _ _ _

X-WING STARFIGHTERS

Find the picture that shows the missing piece of the X-wing. And watch out! The onboard computer is malfunctioning. Don't be fooled by the false fragments it keeps showing the pilot.

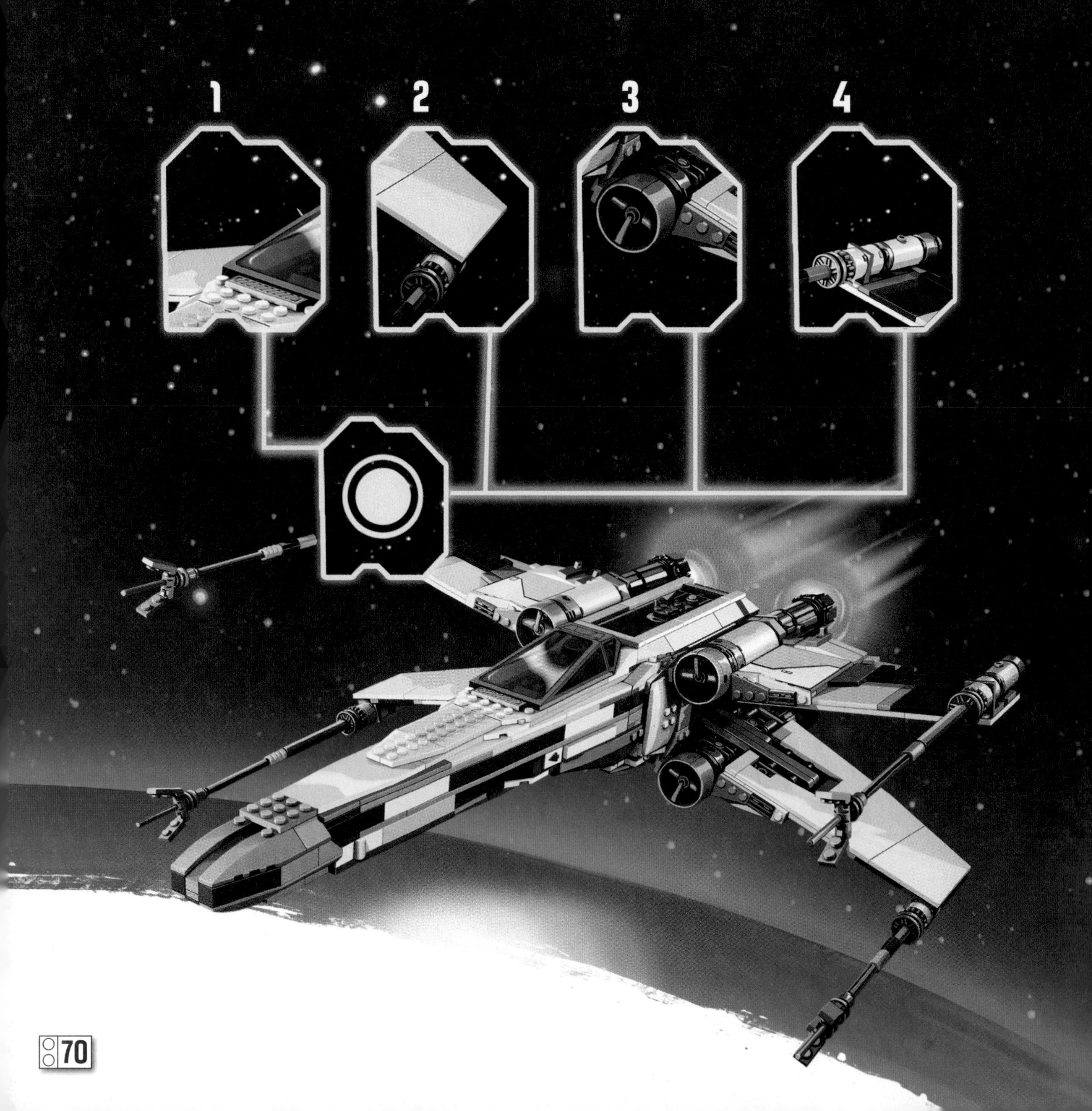

BLAST THE TIE FIGHTERS!

One X-wing found itself in an Empire-controlled space sector. Lead the pilot through the crowded labyrinth so he can blast all the TIE fighters and escape!

THE REBEL PRINCE

Bail Organa was a Senator from Alderaan. Together with a few other trustworthy Senators, they created the Rebel Alliance. Solve the secret codes below to discover Bail Organa's allies, as well as the name of his adopted daughter.

1.

2.

3.

Key:

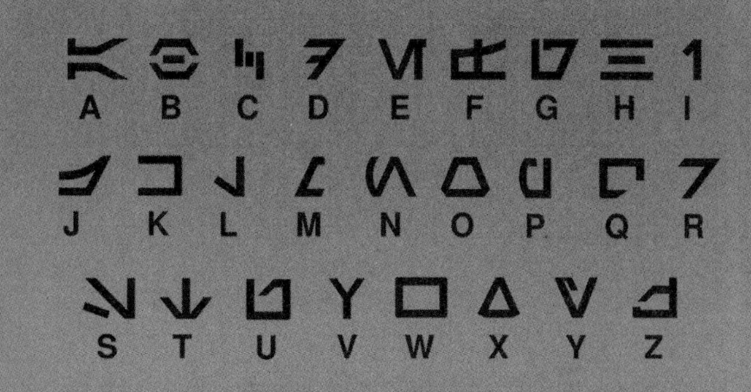

JEDI FORCE FACT

Bail Organa was the owner of the powerful *Tantive IV* spaceship, also used by his daughter.

SECURITY CODE

The starfighters launched from the rebel base on Yavin 4. Help the guard close the base entries by completing the Sudoku security code. Remember: The symbols may not appear twice in any row or column.

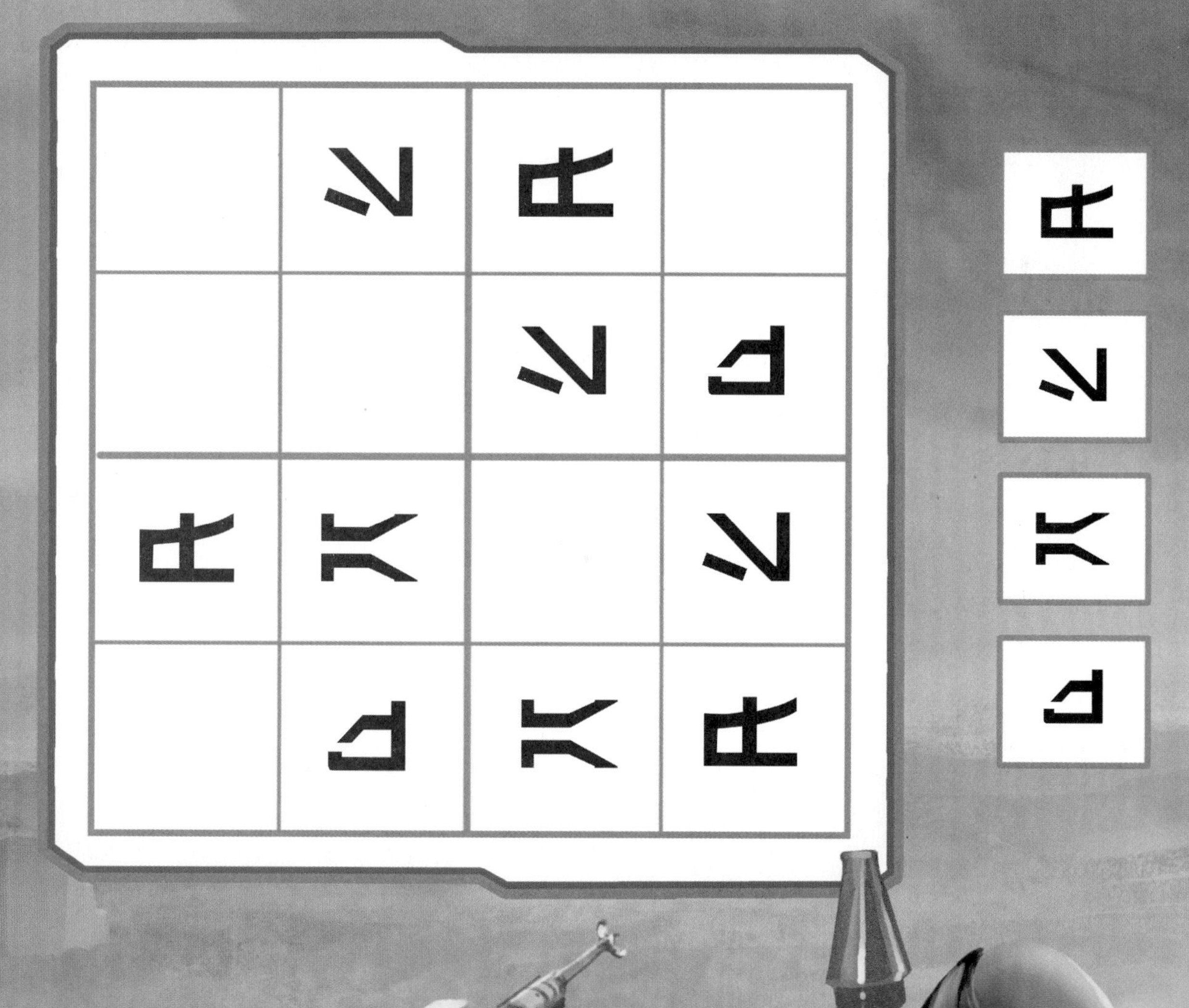

A SMALL PROBLEM

WHAT IS YOUR POSITION? WE DON'T SEE YOU ON THE RADAR.

WHAT DO YOU MEAN "OUR POSITION"? HAVE YOU FORGOTTEN ABOUT US?
WE'RE IN LANDING BAY NUMBER 2 . . .

. . . AND WE'VE BEEN WAITING FOR THE FUEL TANKER FOR HOURS!

SPACE DIFFERENCES

X-wings were definitely the best starfighters in the galaxy. Just ask Luke Skywalker and R2-D2!

Can you spot the 5 differences in these two pictures?

JEDI FORCE FACT

Luke Skywalker destroyed the Empire's first superweapon—the Death Star.

BROKEN MACROBINOCULARS

This guard's macrobinoculars must be on the fritz. Maybe it's the ice-cold climate of Hoth? How many times do you need to turn each ring to the right before the guard spies that oncoming AT-AT? Hint: Use the example below to calibrate your turns.

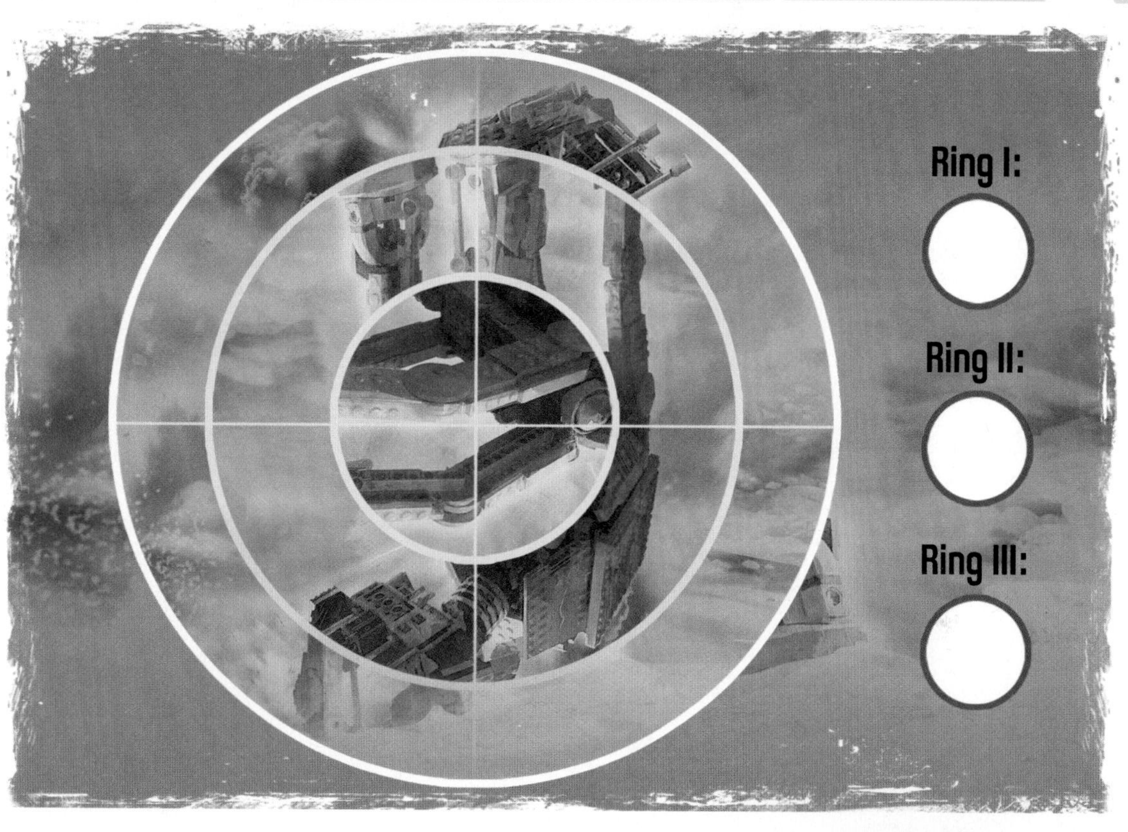

SUPPER

Far away, on the distant planet Hoth, an Imperial snowtrooper squad is scouting the area in search of the rebel base.

AAAH!

¿

SPLAT!

GROOARR!!*
HOTH NEWS
*DARLING! SUPPER'S READY!

FINDERS KEEPERS

Deep in the Outer Rim Territories, a desolate planet named Beheboth was about to get some surprise visitors. A team of rebel X-wing and Y-wing fighters flew over a sea of empty sand dunes.

"Are you sure this is the place, Crix?" asked Princess Leia over the intercom.

"Yeah, it looks deserted down there," agreed Luke Skywalker.

"Well, it is a desert," joked Wedge Antilles.

"That's exactly what the Empire wants you to think," said Crix Madine.

Scattering sand in every direction, the spaceships landed in the middle of nowhere. Leaping out, Luke, Leia, and Wedge followed Crix as he moved up a tall dune. Once on top, Crix pulled out a pair of macrobinoculars. Below them, an Imperial base was hidden under the crushing heat of the sun.

"Is that what I think it is?" asked Leia.

“That base has 500 sandtroopers,” answered Crix. “They are training to survive without water, thrive in the deadly heat, and capture rebels like us.”

“Then what are we doing in their little sandbox?” said Wedge.

“We’re going to take the base from them and capture every last soldier,” said Crix with a diabolical smile. “Follow me.”

Luke, Leia, and Wedge stared at Crix. “You’re joking, right?”

“Nope,” said Crix as he slid back down the hill and found a latch buried in the sand. There was a door underneath. Crix creaked the door open and a passageway appeared before them.

“Ladies first,” said Luke with an uneasy smile.

Leia shook her head, jumped in, and said, “Nervous nerf herders second.”

The hallway was narrow and dark. Once everyone was inside, Crix motioned for them to be quiet.

“This passageway was built for Darth Vader to personally see how the troops performed during training,” whispered Crix as they walked forward. “The troops were too scared when they knew Vader was watching them, so he had this hidden walkway built to watch them without ever being seen.”

"I wish I could never see Darth Vader again," admitted Luke.

"*Shhhh*, we're at our first stop," said Crix.

They were in the back of a kitchen filled with rows of food ready to be served.

"This is no time to eat, Crix!" scolded Leia.

"We're not eating. We're cooking up a little mischief," said Crix. "Let's spice things up."

With that, Crix dumped an entire box of pepper over every plate. Quickly, the group hid as the cafeteria droids came in and brought the food out to the soldiers. As soon as the kitchen doors closed, the sounds of hacking, coughing, and sneezing erupted from the mess hall.

"I guess cracked pepper is all it's cracked up to be!" said Luke. "But annoying these sandtroopers isn't enough. How are we going to catch them, Crix? We need this base for our Outer Rim Territory training facility."

"Then let's go to our second stop," said Crix as the group followed him to a two-way mirror that looked out at an underground barn full of giant, green, lizard-like creatures.

"Are those dewbacks?" asked Wedge.

"You betcha," said Crix. "This is where sandtroopers learn to ride the ugly beasts. But do you wanna know a secret? Dewbacks hate these little suckers." Crix pulled out a jar of several buzzing bugs with vicious fangs.

"Baby skettos!" gasped Luke as he jumped back. "*Ew*, a swarm of those things could eat us alive . . . literally!"

"Yeah, but these babies will give those dewbacks a good scare," said Crix, releasing the skettos into an air duct linked to the barn.

Wedge, Luke, and Leia watched as dewback after dewback suddenly jolted and kicked in fear at the sight and sound of the buzzing skettos. Soon the entire herd was running wild as the sandtroopers were caught in a dewback stampede!

"Well, at least we know what's *bugging* them," said Wedge.

"Now that we have their attention, it's on to stop three," said Crix as he disappeared behind another door.

He was gone for a minute. Then out stepped none other than Darth Vader himself.

"Daddy!" screamed Luke and Leia at the same time, but then Vader pulled off his mask. It was Crix in disguise!

"Vader always keeps a spare outfit at every base," said Crix. "He's a notoriously messy eater. Now, follow me!"

Returning to the cafeteria, Crix walked into the chaotic room with his Darth Vader disguise on. Hordes of sandtroopers were stuck in sneezing fits or surrounded by rampant dewbacks. The giant lizard creatures crashed through the walls of the fort with their riders holding on for dear life.

"Ahem," said Crix, dressed as Vader. The entire room froze with fear. "The Empire needs you immediately. Sandtroopers get outside and into the waiting spaceship. No questions asked! Dewbacks, return to your stalls. Now!"

Instantly, to everyone's surprise, the dewbacks obediently left the room.

Then the sandtroopers lined up and boarded the spaceship outside. Except it wasn't a spaceship. It was a floating prison built by Luke Skywalker. The entire squad was captured.

"Wow! How did you do that?" asked Leia.

"Everybody's crazy about a sharp-dressed man," admitted Crix as he pulled off the Vader mask. "Now, you know what they say: 'Finders keepers, losers weepers.' Call the rest of the rebels. We've got a new home base!"

THE MASTER AND THE STUDENT

The young Luke Skywalker traveled to Dagobah to train under Master Yoda and become a Jedi Knight. Did this awaken the resurgence of the Jedi Order? Only time will tell . . .

Find and count the items that Yoda is controlling with the Force and appear twice.

A PIRATE OR A REBEL?

Han Solo began his pilot career as a smuggler and a pirate. Later, he became one of the Rebellion leaders who helped destroy not one, but both Death Stars.

Do you know what planet Han Solo comes from? Ignore all the digits and decipher the name.

8974C67802345 9R298745EL876L918A

_ _ _ _ _ _ _ _

THE FASTEST IN THE GALAXY

The *Millennium Falcon* was a modified YT-1300 Corellian freighter, and one of the fastest spaceships in terms of hyperspace travel. This ship and its daring crew played a major role during the Galactic Civil War.

All of the *Millennium Falcon*'s pictures are missing a different piece. Look closely and circle what's out of place.

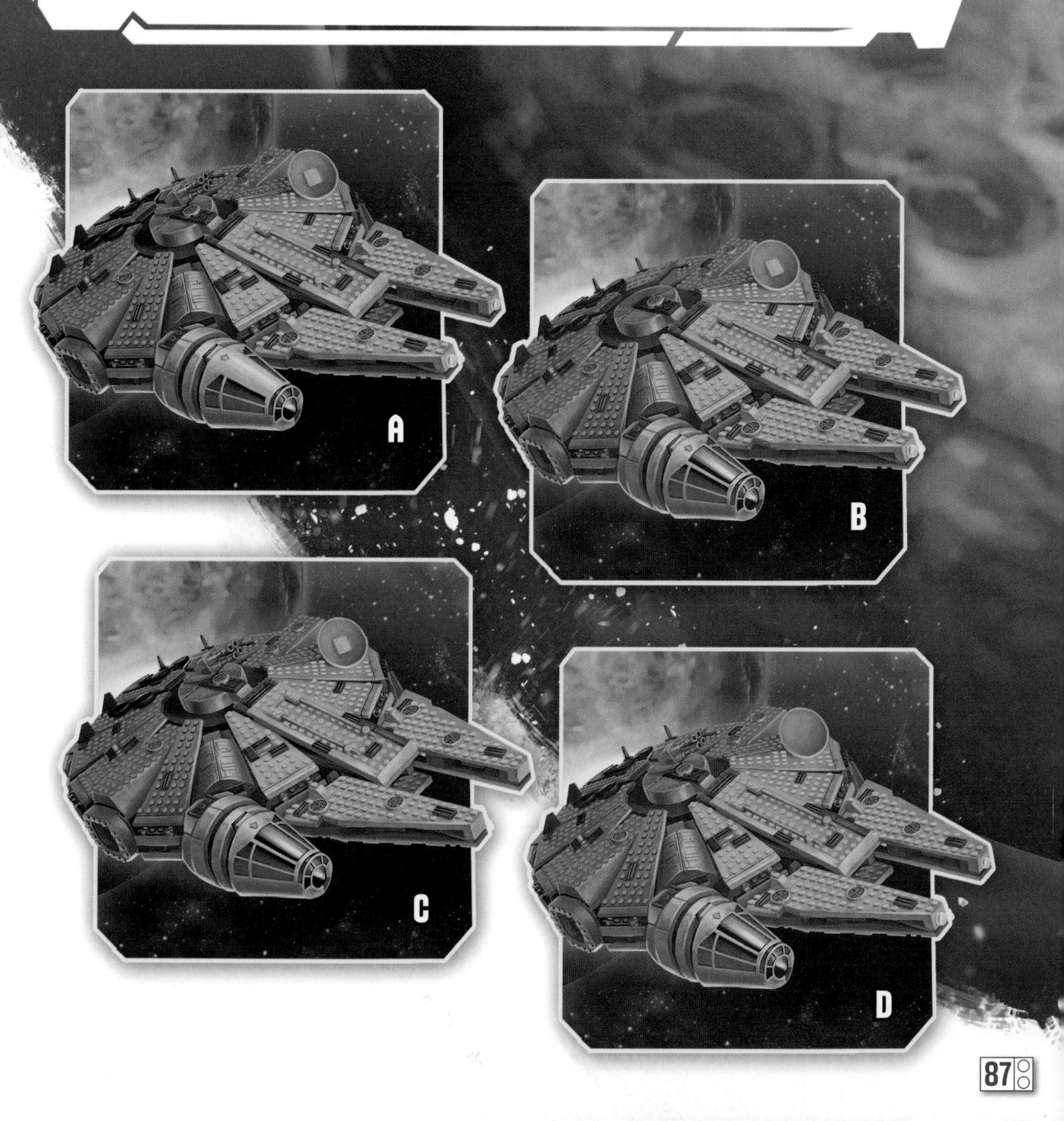

THE CALM DROID

C-3PO was a protocol droid who never wanted any trouble. The problem was, trouble always seemed to find him.

Find the two identical pictures of C-3PO.

R2-D2'S MISSION

The brave droid, R2-D2, was trying to save his friends from Darth Vader's trap when he ran into trouble with the cables.

Help R2-D2 rewire the security system by writing the number of elements in the correct places.

JEDI DEFENSE

When Luke Skywalker and Boba Fett were battling on Tatooine, it looked like the bounty hunter had the young Jedi trapped. Help defend Luke against Boba Fett's attacks. Write the correct symbols in the empty boxes.

ATTACK		DEFENSE	
△	Single shot	+	Dodge single shot
○	Volley shot from the left	π	Dodge volley shot from the left
□	Volley shot from the top	∼	Dodge volley shot from the top
⏢	Single shot from the right	⌒	Block single shot from the right

SURPRISE ATTACK

On the forest moon of Endor, Imperial biker scouts were protecting the shield generator. But when they discovered rebel commandos on a mission to shut down the generator, the stormtroopers scatterd to warn the Empire. Help Luke navigate the labyrinth on his speeder bike to stop the last stormtrooper from giving away the rebels' plans!

REBEL FLEET

MILLENNIUM FALCON

MANUFACTURER: CORELLIAN ENGINEERING CORPORATION
MODEL: YT-1300
CLASS: LIGHT FREIGHTER

LENGTH: 34.75 M
WIDTH: 20 M
ENGINE UNIT: 2 GIRODYNE SRB42 SUBLIGHT ENGINES
MAXIMUM ACCELERATION: 3,000 G
SPEED IN ATMOSPHERE: 650 MPH
SPEED IN SPACE: 75 MGL

ARMAMENTS: 2 QUAD LASER CANNONS AG-2G
1 CONCEALED BLASTECH AX-108 SURFACE-DEFENSE BLASTER CANNON
2 4-MISSILE ARAKYD ST2 CONCUSSION MISSILE TUBES (REMOVED AROUND 24 YEARS AFTER THE BATTLE OF YAVIN.)
ANTIPERSONNEL BEAM EMITTER
HIGH-POWER MARK VII TRACTOR BEAM GENERATOR

DECODE:

REBEL QUIZ

Are you ready for a short quiz? Choose the correct answer to each question and see if you are a true rebel genius. And don't be persuaded by the dark side to look back at the previous pages before you finish. May the Force be with you.

1. The full name of the Rebellion is:
   a. The Rebel Alliance
   b. The Anti-Empire Alliance
   c. The Anti-Dark Force Alliance

2. Rogue Squadron is an armada of pilots that fly:
   a. A-wings
   b. X-wings
   c. TIE fighters

3. With whom did Bail Organa create the Rebel Alliance?
   a. A few kings of other planets
   b. A few Senators faithful to the Republic
   c. A few pirate ship captains

4. Who destroyed the first Death Star?
   a. Han Solo
   b. Obi-Wan Kenobi
   c. Luke Skywalker

5. Who was the owner of the ship *Tantive IV*?
   a. Bail Organa
   b. Darth Vader
   c. Lando Calrissian

6. Hoth is famous for:
   a. Its good food and sunny weather
   b. Incredibly cold temperatures
   c. Being covered with bogs

7. Han Solo started his pilot career as:
   a. A smuggler and a pirate
   b. A cook on a cruise ship
   c. An experimental test pilot

ANSWERS

Pg. 68 The Rebel Army

D

Pg. 69 Rogue Squadron

WEDGE ANTILLES

Pg. 70 X-wing Starfighters

4

Pg. 71 BLAST The Tie Fighters!

Pg. 72 The Rebel Prince

1. MON MOTHMA
2. PADME AMIDALA
3. LEIA ORGANA

Pg. 73 Security Code

Pg. 76 Space Differences

Pg. 77 Broken Macrobinoculars

Ring I: Ring II: Ring III:

Pg. 85 The Master and the Student

Pg. 86 A Pirate or a Rebel?

CORELLIA

Pg. 87 The Fastest in the Galaxy

Pg. 88 THE CALM DROID

Pg. 89 R2-D2'S Mission

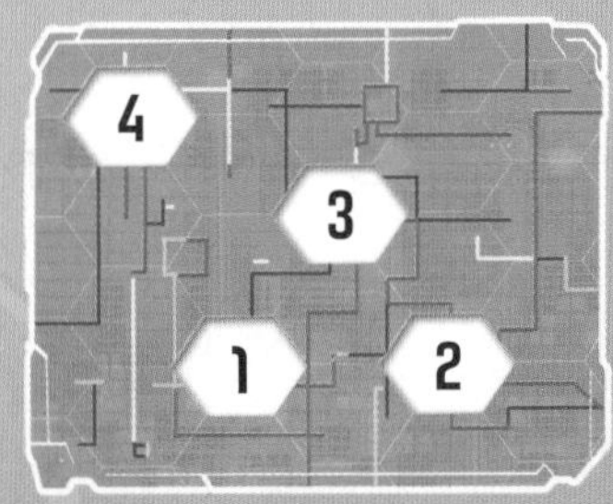

Pg. 91 Surprise Attack

Pg. 90 Jedi Defense

Pgs. 94–95 Rebel Quiz

1 – a, 2 – b, 3 – b, 4 – c, 5 – a, 6 – b, 7 – a.